Unplanned

Sacred Sexuality, Black & African American Erotica,

Forbidden Seducing Short Stories For Adult, First Time,

Menage Age Gap

Lana Kendra

This is a work of fiction; names, characters, places, and incidents are either the product of the author's imagination or are used fictitiously, and any resemblance to actual people, living or dead, business establishments, events, or locales is entirely coincidental.

This e-book is for your personal use only and may not be resold or given to anyone else. If you want to give this book to someone else, please buy an extra copy for each person. If you're reading this book and didn't buy it, or if it wasn't bought for your personal use only, go back to your favorite ebook retailer and buy your copy. Thank you for acknowledging this author's efforts.

Table of Contents

Content Warning

Due to its sexual content, this book is only for those over the age of legal adulthood. There are some topics with a lot of foul language. All of the characters are at least eighteen years old.

Introduction

Are you in search of an exciting and thrilling book to read? Look no further than this extensive collection of Erotic Suspense book. I offer a wide range of genres, including Romantic Erotica, Fantasy, and Urban BDSM Fiction, to cater to even the most discerning reader. Whether you enjoy Anthologies, Westerns, or Paranormal Romance, I have something to suit your taste. My collection also includes Poetic Folklore, Interracial, Black & African American Literary Criticism, and Gothic Horror for those who crave a deeper and darker reading experience. If you're interested in Futuristic, LGBTQ+, Short Stories, or Lesbian literature, my diverse range of options will keep you captivated. Additionally, I offer Humorous, Victorian, New Adult, and College Women's Psychological Mysteries for those seeking a lighter but equally engaging read. Furthermore, My Fairy Tale Collections,

Transgender, Contemporary Western, Bisexual, and Poetry genres will transport you to different worlds and explore a variety of themes. For my Teen and Young Adult readers, I have a selection of European Geography, Cultures, eBooks, Loners, Outcasts, Mythology, Folk Tales, and much more. With such a wide array of options to choose from, you'll never run out of thrilling and enchanting stories to immerse yourself in.

This is a fictional story with tricky moves and plan. This is a story that will captivate your mind and turn on your fantasy gear for your long erotic desire. Enjoy the sexual tentions embedded in this story.

It is important to emphasize that this content is exclusively intended for individuals who are 18 years of age or older.

Unplanned

The sun was blazing at me in the brilliant morning light when I woke up. I rolled onto my face, squinting my eyes tight and moaning. My eyes were still being tugged by sleep, drawing me into dreamland—that warm, dark realm. However, I knew I had to get up. I got out of bed slowly and checked the time on my clock. It stated 8:37. Whoa, I slept in later than I had intended to. I evaluated myself by glancing in the mirror that served as my closet door. With my messy dark brown hair, I reached up and smoothed my fingers through it. I could feel my morning passion squeezing through my boxer shorts. It didn't seem to solidify until I stood up and it began to swing back and forth.

I walked over to my drawers and took a few items out. I approached the door that separated my room from the restroom. My bedroom and my stepsister Rosemary's bedrooms were connected by a bathroom due to the layout of the house plan. We share a bathroom, which has worked out really well so far. Occasionally, though, I'll discover a hair the color of amber on my towel or in the shower. She is about 5'4" with somewhat small breasts, but her porcelain legs and ass have drawn the attention of many boys. I have never purposefully peeked in on my sister, but I have occasionally caught a glimpse of her skin and have been turned on, but I'm not a pervert; I wouldn't do that.

After entering the bathroom and turning on the shower, I undressed, still feeling the hardness of the morning; I gave it a good few strokes when I heard the sound of the door opening.

My stepbrother, Alex, has been living in our spare bedroom since he was fifteen years old. His family had perished in a fire at their family reunion, and he and his mother had been the only ones to survive. I woke up this morning having slept like a rock, my back deliciously warm. I sat up and turned to look at the 22-year-old person who was sharing my bed with me. Her blonde hair spread out on my pillow, she looked more like an angel than my cousin as she slept.

My father raised me until I was fifteen years old, when he married Christina, Alex's mother. She is the most lovely woman I have ever met, and I have come to accept her as my mother, but it isn't the same connection that I have with my dad. We have always been close. My mother had died giving birth to me, and for that I am eternally grateful.

As I dragged my drawers open to find the clothes I thought would work for today, I heard a rustle in the covers behind me and turned to see Sandra sitting up in bed, only her panties and a tank top on, her nipples hard and protruding through the thin material of her shirt; if there was one thing that everyone knew about Sandra, it was that she was not afraid to show off her skin, which at times made her appear slutty or even lesbian, but that was just the way she was.

"How are you doing?"With a hint of sleepiness lingering in her voice, she questioned.

I said to her, "Just going to take a quick shower." She got up, went to her suitcase, and took out her clothing, choosing a tank top and a pair of shorts that seemed a little too short for my taste. She then placed her clothes on top of my dresser and removed her tank top.

Many a male had dreamed of caressing those magnificent things, her enormous breasts with their boldly protruding nipples; she gave them a fun little jiggle, acknowledging that she was proud of the set she had, then reached down and removed her panties.

"When did that occur?"With a gesture to the silky skin over her vagina, I questioned.

"I got it waxed last week," she responded, "hurt like hell, but it sure looks good; and the guys like it."

While contemplating this, I failed to hear the sound of the

shower starting up. After getting dressed and entering the restroom, I saw Alex standing there with his cock facing me and holding a large, impressive-looking cock—at least seven inches long.

He turned away from me and attempted to cover himself with a towel from the rack, and I turned tail and jumped back in to my room, and there was a moment of bewilderment before either of us fully noticed that one was naked with a boner.

"What took place?Sandra questioned while putting on her panties.

I hesitantly said, "Well, I walked in to the bathroom, but Alex was in there already. He was completely nude and, um... He possessed a boner."

"Really?Incredulously, she exclaimed, "How big was he?""

"Well... About seven inches? Why?"

"Because; he's kinda cute."

My brain was burned by her.

"How dare I? You have a cousin named him! My sibling!"I exclaimed, startled.

"STEP-brother!"I said," she said.

Now that my stepbrother was beautiful, my brain was working nonstop to process this information.

Rose suggested, "Just think about it. He's a runner and a swimmer, so his body is well-toned." At times, he acts like a true gentleman and is quite kind. He's a pretty handsome guy. You simply find it difficult to regard him that way since you now consider him to be your brother. But that's not how he sees you."

"What are you trying to say?"

"What I mean is, he looks at you the same way he would look at any other cute girl he sees," she stated angrily. "But he plays it cool, not moving because he fears it might cause problems." Tell me, have you truly not noticed that he occasionally looks at you?"

Upon further reflection, he did occasionally give me a strange look; there was something about his eyes that I couldn't quite put my finger on.

"All right, so... I've been looked at weird before," I remarked.

"AHA! You are aware of what I mean!"Now start preparing breakfast before your mother wakes up," she yelled. You are aware that she would value that.

My head was whirling as I walked out of the room. My cousin had just brought it up, but I was having trouble understanding. Even if what she was discussing was quite strange... In several ways, it was accurate.

My brother was a handsome man. I know that many of my pals felt the same way. Ashley, one of them, even went out with him for a few weeks. Still. That brother of yours is still that brother. Correct?

After half an hour, I prepared a steaming hot breakfast for everyone who was willing to sit down at the dining room table. My favorite breakfast combination is French toast, eggs, and bacon, so that's what I made. About five minutes before breakfast was done, my stepmom had come outside, grabbed it, and quickly left for work.

"Bye honey. Enjoy the week off okay? I should be home around 10 tonight your father won't be back until tomorrow night." She said.

"All right, have a great day at work!" I answered. She then left through the door.

For her age, my stepmother was an attractive woman. Her dark hair fell down to the small of her back, and she stood five feet three inches tall, quite short but with huge breasts and a shapely physique; I knew from what I had heard that several women her age envied her young looks.

Hearing the front door close and her car pull away, I turned to see Alex heading down the stairs. He entered the kitchen, took a plate from the cabinet, and sat down, looking expectantly at me as he did so. I pulled my chair back and sat down to watch Sandra come down the stairs.

Coming downstairs, I saw that Rosemary had made French toast with eggs and bacon for breakfast, and that Alex had given me a beating. As we started eating, I could feel the tension between Rose and Alex building, so I left the room to give them some space and time to themselves.

"I need to go to the bathroom guys, I'll be back in just a minute." I said.

I got up and went to the bathroom by walking down the corridor.

Rose broke the ice first, but I still found myself pausing and listening to what they had to say.

"Look Alex, I really didn't mean to barge in on you like

that," she stated before starting to speak quickly. "I wasn't expecting to walk in on you naked; much less with a boner, and then you caught me by surprise, and I couldn't help staring because.."

"Look, Rose, accidents happen," he interrupted her. You didn't mean it, I know that. Do you recall a month or two ago when I happened to walk in on you getting dressed?"

She answered, "That was different; I was in my underwear."

"Still," he said.

I had to admit, all of this was turning me on a bit. Then, my dirty mind began to work on a dirty, sensual idea, and she had the perfect way to spin it.

After breakfast was finished and the dishes were done, I headed upstairs while my lustful thoughts continued to swirl around my scheme.

"Hey, I have to go check on a friend of mine in town. Do

you recall Alicia? I'll be back in a moment, okay? She was in a vehicle accident a few days ago.Rose said something that I heard.

Alex answered, "Alright. Do you know where my computer's charger is?"

She said, "I had to borrow it; it's in my room."

"Alright, I'll get it after I'm finished loading the dishwasher." He replied.

This conversation put my plan into overdrive, so I waited until I heard Rose leave before entering her room and getting completely nude. I was thinking about my sneaky little plan, so it felt amazing to get some relief down there. I started rubbing myself, starting around the outside edges of my pussy lips and working my way in. I let out a low moan, because it felt so good. Before I knew it, I had slipped a finger in and was experiencing intense pleasure. I was almost completely lost in my lustful daze, and I was moving my body all over in pleasure.

I kid you not, his mouth dropped open as he regained consciousness and spun around, walking back through the door and shutting it behind him. I heard him walk across the hall and shut the door behind him, and I knew he must have a raging boner by now. I saw the door open and Alex move into the room, and the look of surprise on his face was priceless and turned me on even more. He stopped and stared at me; his eyes combing my skin from my face to my boobs until coming to rest at the place I was rubbing between my spread legs.

I stood up and peered in Rose's floor-length mirror on her room's wall. Masturbating had added some color to my face; I looked pretty damn good. Most boys would kill to get their hands on me. A few boys had fucked me before, but nothing had exited me like this. This was new and uncharted territory. I was ready. I stayed where I was and continued to plow Alex's thick cock inside me. I climaxed with hurricane force arching my back off the bed.

I opened my door and slipped down the hall to his, listening and hearing the telltale sign of him jacking off. I loved it, so much so that I opened his door and walked in, still naked, to find him lying on his bed with his dick in his hand. He quickly hid under his blankets and yelled at me, embarrassed. I had never felt so slutty and sexy before.

"Sandra! How in the hell are you in here? Leave now!"

He gave me an uncomfortable look as I walked over to his bed, ignored him, and put my hand on the tent he had made with his hard-on.

Is this a pleasant feeling?"I inquired.

He tried to hide it, but I moved his hands away from it and he stopped trying. There was no reaction, so I took the initiative and pulled the covers aside, revealing his stiff cock to the world.

"It's okay, it's quite normal," I reassured him. You became

excited when you witnessed a young, attractive female caressing herself. You'd like to obtain some relief right now."

Having stated that, I put my hand around his shaft and began to very slowly raise and lower my hands.

I drooled, "Maybe I can help you with that."

I could tell he was enjoying it as I planted a kiss on the top of his cock, causing an unconscious tremor to run through his body.

My mind was at war; on the one side was the shouting side of Reason, and on the other was my cousin, who was stroking me and trying to help me with my "problem." Holy Fuck, that felt amazing.

"Stupid, what the fuck are you doing? For heaven's sake, she is your cousin! This is incorrect!"

You can probably guess which side was winning. However, the side of reason was quite stubborn and in a desperate attempt to come to the surface, my mouth moved without first consulting my brain. This was my lust-filled side, the side that was commenting on how good it felt and wondering how far she would take this.

"My cousin is you. We have no business doing this. That is to say... Oh.

That side of reason was immediately crushed, and I chided myself inside for uttering something with absolutely no force behind it.

She responded in a very seductive voice, "I don't think you want me to stop."

I don't know whether you can grin while doing something like that, but she sure tried. She proceeded to suck my cock in to her mouth, a little bit at a moment, and after saying that, she took the head of my prick in to her mouth, prompting me to release a tiny gasp.

"Oh, please, Lord!"I cried out.

I brushed the blonde hair around her ear so that I could look at her face as she went down on me, and that's when she really started going down on me. She sucked me almost all the way down and started striving to take my full length within the next fifteen seconds. Her nose was brushing in to my pubic hair and my cock head was brushing the back of her throat.

I shouted, "Oh yea! Oh God, I'm gonna cum." Yes! Yes! Fuuuck!"

When I hosed the back of her throat with my come, she took it all down, every last drop. She was so beautiful that she gave it one more kiss, right on top, and got up. I don't think I had ever cum so much before.

She kissed the top of my head and added, "Maybe we can do this again sometime."

She was a great girl, and I would always remember that she left me in a drunken daze of perfect ecstasy as she went out my door, her beautiful ass swaying as she walked.

I was curious about what was going on between Sandra and Alex, but I couldn't quite put my finger on it. They kept stealing glances at each other, especially Alex, as if they were members of a secret society that I was unaware of. I wish I knew what it was.

"How was Alicia doing?"May I ask?" Alex inquired.

Yes, she was alright. The physician announced that she would be released to her parents this evening."

"Well that's good."

"Hey, let me hop in the shower, will you please?"

Yes, that's alright. Actually, my plan was to visit Mica's house across the street."

"All right. Enjoy yourself."

I sprinted upstairs, entered the bathroom, undressed, turned on the water, and looked at my reflection in the mirror. I was happy with my appearance; sure, my boobs could have been bigger, but my butt was fine, and I had a pussy that people had told me was beautiful; my boobs had the most perky, sensitive nipples that, with just a gentle touch, sent tiny bolts of electricity racing through me.

Satisfied that the water was hot enough by now, I turned away from my reflection and hopped in the shower. The water was much hotter than I had expected, so I gave a little yelp as it hit my skin. I backed out of the water's stream and reached around to turn the heat down some. Once the water had cooled enough for my liking, I stepped in and wet my body in the warm stream. My hair was an amber brown color and had a way wavy, which was quite pretty. I had been told since I was a little girl that I had the most beautiful hair.

A creak went off, and I quickly poked my head through the shower curtain to see who was invading my privacy. Sandra was standing there, nude. That creak, I realized, was the sound of the door opening.

"I also need to get a shower. Would you mind if I joined you?"May I ask?" she inquired.

"Don't you think this is a little too huge for us?"I asked hurriedly.

She shook her head, explaining that we had been showering together since we were twelve. Our family wasn't very wealthy, and our water heater had broken, leaving only enough hot water for one person to shower, so we had to share the shower. We discovered that showering together wasn't as embarrassing as we had thought, and after that first time it became a kind of regular thing. It gave us some alone time to talk about things we couldn't discuss with our parents, and they weren't concerned about us being lesbian or anything because we had dated boys throughout middle and high school. However, there had been a few occasions when we had experimented with each other while sharing a shower or a bed, so we had stopped doing that since she graduated.

"Alright," I replied, "I suppose you could join me since nobody's here."

Her golden hair clinging to her back and shoulders, she looked stunningly beautiful as the water cascaded down her breasts and abdomen, and she grinned as she bounded over to the shower and widened the gap I had made in the shower curtain so she could climb in with me. There was a brief moment of shuffling as we adjusted to there being two people in the shower before I stepped aside so she could get herself wet.

"Could you please lather me up?With a knowing smirk on her face, she questioned.

I was startled when I felt a hand caress my butt as I spun around to pick up the body wash off the tub's edge behind me.

She exclaimed, "You have a beautiful ass, Rose."

"Well. I said, "Thank you," and then I poured some body wash into my palm.

She turned around and I began rubbing the soap into her back after I had lathered her back in it and then softly rubbed it into her ass.

"Hmm. It feels good," she remarked.

She gasped a little as I touched her pussy, and I kept going down till I had to sit on my knees in the tub's bottom.

"Sorry"

"No, you're alright. It was satisfying!"

We both let out screams of surprise as I moved down her legs, lathering up the front and backs. I believe she pushed her butt backwards a little bit when I stood up because my tits brushed against it.

I said, not sure what to do next.

"Now for the front I guess."

I massaged down her arms, across her shoulders, and across her collarbone before focusing on her boobs as she turned to face me.

It's alright. You are able to touch them," she chuckled.

She let out a little groan as I worked the soap into her huge breasts. I pretended not to hear her, and as I worked my way down, I lathered her hips and stomach. I thought she leaned a little closer to me during this process.

When she was done rinsing off, I remarked, "Okay, your turn."

She took some soap in her palm and began with the front, massaging the tits till a gasp escaped my lips, just as I did. She started with the arms and worked her way up to the chest.

"Hmm. Nonetheless delicate." She spoke while squeezing them just enough to cause another gasp.

She began by massaging my hips and abs, then moved on to my legs, paying close attention to the insides of my thighs. She moved her hand to my pussy after finishing my legs. She rubbed it thoroughly.

"Oh!" I said, astonished.

"Mm," she said.

She got to her feet and gave me a direct look. She reached through my arms to give me a kind of hug and began caressing my back.

"What are you doing?" I inquired, not knowing the circumstances.

"I just felt like trying something new." she stated.

She began massaging my back with soap, and even though I wasn't sure, I went with it. Her huge breasts had drawn me in even more, pressing them against my smaller ones. It felt very wonderful, I had to admit, and I was starting to feel a little turned on. She leaned down, father, and gave my ass a good squeeze while rubbing soap in it.

She said, "Feels nice,..."

She leaned down after that and gave me a kiss that no cousin should ever give. A mouth-filling kiss that drew me in and held me in. A kiss with such sensuality. I adored it.

I started massaging Rose's ass as I kissed her. She wrapped her arms around to lay her hands on mine, welcoming it. We kissed passionately and lustfully, pressing our bodies close to each other as though to unite, till we were ravenous for each other. I trapped her against the cool wall. I broke off our kiss and ran my lips along her neck, working my way up to her collarbone. She put her hand between our bodies and started rubbing her thumb and fingertip along my left nipple.

I moved away from her and covered her right breast with my lips, prompting her to gasp out and then moan. I was driven insane as her free hand descended to my drenched pussy and began rubbing my clit. I tore us apart once more.

I grabbed her right leg and brought it up to my hip. Next, I lifted my right leg and set it on the tub's edge. We began grinding against each other as soon as I positioned my pussy against hers. Along with each other, we were squealing and groaning with wonderful joy as the water's steam surrounded us. I gave her a hungry kiss while the shower's water jets sprayed across my face. I could sense Rose's breath quickening, knowing she was about to have her own climax as well.

"Oh my goodness, Sandra! God, it really is! Sandra, that is accurate.Ah, ah, ahhh.

Simultaneously, she reached her peak. We shook, ground, and caressed each other while the force of our climax rocked us, our pleasurable screams resonating off the shower walls.

About 3:45 in the afternoon, I returned from Mica's house,

and as soon as I opened the door, I could sense a change in the situation. It wasn't because I noticed Rose and Sandra cuddling up on the couch to watch a movie. It was because they were cuddling with each other in their underpants. When I entered the living room, I saw that they were enjoying a romantic film. The moment I placed my luggage on the counter, they both straightened up immediately.

"Ah! "Alex!" Rose murmured, hastily pulling a blanket over her head.

Sandra pretended not to care that she was only wearing her panties. She gave me a long, hard look before she spoke.

"Alex, come sit down over here I want to talk to you for a minute." Says she.

I moved over and took a seat in the armchair next to the couch. They were watching a movie, so she grabbed up the TV remote and switched it off.

"I told Rose about what you and I did earlier." Coolly, she said.

I was so embarrassed that my eyebrows shot up to the celling and blood rushed to my face.

"Don't feel ashamed," she replied, giving Rose a wink. "Rose and I did a few things of our own, didn't we Rose?"

"Well. Yes, we did. With hesitation, she spoke.

"And I was thinking that all three of us could have some fun." Sandra laughed and said.

"Uh...what do you mean?" I mentioned that I already had some thoughts.

"Well come on up to Rose's Bedroom and we'll show you!" she replied.

Grabbing Rose's hand, she helped her get out of her seat. They ran up the stairs together, and I heard Rose's chamber door close. I pondered over it for a moment there. Was I prepared for this at all? During the talk, I had developed a hard on, and that was definitely influencing my ideas. I got up from my chair and headed up the stairs without giving it any thought. I paused at the door and inhaled deeply; this is who I am. From here on out, there was no going back. I then lowered my hand and pulled open the door. I was unsure of the number of others it would open.

Looking around the room, I noticed the girls kissing each other in a tangle on the bed. I definitely had a hard-on now, if I didn't already. Their hair was a tangle of yellow and amber-brown, and their limbs were disorganized. They were kissing so intensely and intimately that they were blind to my presence. Or perhaps they did and were indifferent to it.

In any case, I arrived and took a seat at the foot of the bed. They became aware of this.

"Well look who decided to join us!" Sandra remarked jokingly.

She broke away from Rose and moved across to sit on the other side of the bed. She swung her leg across my lap and I had to sit back on my hands. She continued, taking two handfuls of my shirt, "I've been waiting for this for a long time."

Her mouth met mine, hard and sensitive at the same moment as she leaned in to kiss. She leaned closer to me as I gave her a kiss in return. I collapsed back onto the bed after putting my hands up around her. Our lips became closer, and before long, I felt someone pull my shirt over my head—not Sandra. Keeping Sandra on my lap, I sat up and noticed that my stepsister was sitting to my left, holding my shirt. It was the loveliest thing ever, and it made me want to kiss her till my lips hurt. I reached out to touch her, but I was unable. She closed the space and I placed my lips on hers, choosing to go with it. I felt electric shocks shoot through me so strongly that was surprising Sandra wasn't shocked. I drew her in closer by putting an arm around her waist. She kissed me more firmly and placed a warm hand on my chest.

Sandra had begun to move back and forth on my restricted dick, leaving a wet mark on my khaki shorts as she felt my raging boner beneath her. Sandra got to her feet as our kisses grew sexier, but Rosemary moved to take her position on my lap and shoved me onto my back. I lowered my hands and began massaging her stunning posterior. I felt Sandra tug on my shorts at that moment.

She remarked, "I don't think you'll be needing these!" as she removed them.

"And I don't think you'll be needing this." As I took Rose's bra off, I said to her.

It settled on my chest after sliding down her arms. As I stared at her nude tits, I was astounded. Although Sandra's were not the largest I had ever seen, they were so adorable and well-proportioned that they made my heart skip a beat.

"You like them?" she inquired with anticipation.

I was only able to nod. She leaned in to kiss me, laughing at my incapacity to speak. Sandra tugged Rose's panties all the way down to her knees just before our lips met once more. Rose gasped in astonishment.

"I apologize, Rose. Sandra said, "I was so excited to see that gorgeous pussy again."

She remarked in a very seductive way, "Well, everyone can see mine, so why don't you show off yours?"

Sandra stepped back from us and parted her feet a little. Without bending at the knee, she then pulled her panties down to her ankles. That's how hot she was.

I wanted Alex in me more than anything since he had been so hot when he was kissing me. At that moment, I wanted to fuck my stepbrother more than I had ever wanted to fuck a boy. I completely undid my underwear after rolling off of him. He sat up, staring at Sandra as she turned around and flashed her enormous breasts without a bra.

At that moment, I witnessed Alex get up and undress as well. When his erect cock got thus close to me, it seemed even bigger. I dropped on my knees and put his cockhead in my mouth without even thinking.

"Oh my god," he exclaimed.

Sandra approached him from the side and remarked, "You enjoy that, don't you? Like I did previously, is your sister putting your enormous dick in her little mouth? I believe that.

"Are you ready to fuck her now? I'm sucking her lovely pussy, and you want to fuck her too, is that correct?

"Mm hm." In a stupor, he said.

"Stand up Rose." Sandra gave an order, saying, "Do this for me. You take a seat on the bed. Alex was shoved onto the bed's back by her. She turned to face me, "And you know what to do from there."

I also did. I positioned myself over him, trapping his penis in between us. I positioned his dick at my opening and slipped down on top of it after getting up on my knees.

"Oh my gosh! You feel enormous!" I said.

He said, "And you're so fucking tight!"

I began to slowly roll over on top of him and began to rise and fall. We were traveling rather swiftly, and we could hear the sounds of our irrational reactions. I was about to fall on Alex when I felt Sandra lick me. As he fucked me, she started licking me from behind! I had my first climax not too long after.

Alex then withdrew from me. He rolled onto my back, slipped in close to me, and pushed my legs back up to my head. I gasped and said, "That." Feels so damned good. Alright!"

Sandra then leaned over me and covered my face with her pussy.

"Will you handle this for me?" she inquired.

I got to work liking and mopping up her pussy's fluids right away.

"Alex, do you like that? Fucking her cousin and your stepsister? Well? Will you be getting married soon? Will you be putting your cum on your tiny little sister? Is that accurate? stated Sandra.

Alex leaned down and stroked my tits, releasing one of my legs in the process. His nipple rubbing drove me insane. Almost all of us arrived at the same time. pushing one another to the limit. The whole house was filled with our squeals and groans of delight. Alex made me feel full. His warm fluid swirling inside of me felt so nice. I had developed a hitherto undiscovered fondness for my stepbrother. I was confident that we would keep coming up with new methods to make each other happy. And all of it was made possible by my cousin's sultry scheme.

Acknowledgments

The Glory of this book's success goes to God Almighty and my beautiful Family, Fans, Readers & well-wishers, Customers, and Friends for their endless support and encouragement.

About The Author

I've spent nearly a decade penning romantic novels. As a passionate writer of erotica, I craft dark, romantic erotica. Anime Naked Truth Se of Sacred Sexuality: Forbidden Seducing Short Stories of an Erotica Nude Sexy Girl Poster. Alongside Erotic Mystery Fiction, Victorian Erotica Sex, Black & African American Erotica, Euthanasia, Daddy Teaching, Forced Domination, Alpha Monster Cuckold, and BDSM for Adults, there's an Erotic Fiction in Kinky Family. I write dark, sensual romance because I adore the power of darkness and everything that it entails. Romance novels have always been my favorite kind of books, and now I'm writing them. The idea that you will like reading and enjoying my fiction as much as I enjoy pushing the frontiers of sexual pleasure in my writing thrills me more than anything else.